Ingrid Hess

Walk in Peace

Ingrid Hess

Herald
Press

Scottdale, Pennsylvania
Waterloo, Ontario

Library of Congress Cataloging-in-Publication Data
Hess, Ingrid.
Walk in peace / Ingrid Hess.
    p. cm.
ISBN 978-0-8361-9469-2 (pbk. : alk. paper)
1. Peace–Religious aspects–Christianity–Juvenile literature.
2. God–Love–Juvenile literature.
3. Children–Prayers and devotions.
I. Title.
  BT736.4.H475 2009
  242'.62–dc22

                        2008047275

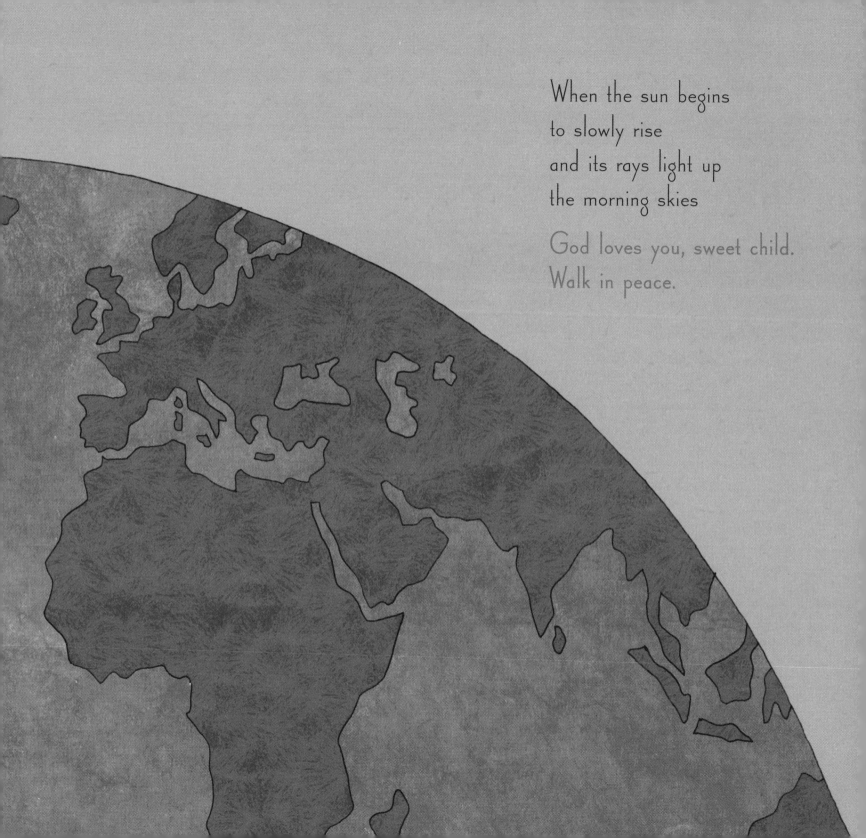

When the sun begins
to slowly rise
and its rays light up
the morning skies

God loves you, sweet child.
Walk in peace.

When the rooster wakes
'cause it sees the sun
and it crows to all
that the day's begun

God loves you, sweet child.
Walk in peace.

When garden flowers
greet the breaking day
with their dewy blooms
and their gentle sway

God loves you, sweet child.
Walk in peace.

When you wake and remember
a dream you had
so you rush to tell
your mom and dad,

or when teeth are brushed
and you're finally dressed
and your hair is braided
and you look your best

God loves you, sweet child.
Walk in peace.

When the marsh awakes
from its night of sleep
and the dragonflies buzz
and the bullfrogs leap

God loves you, sweet child.
Walk in peace.

When the laundry's up
on the backyard line
where it hangs to dry
in the warm sunshine

God loves you, sweet child.
Walk in peace.

When your breakfast's done
and all put away
and it's finally time
to run and play,

or when the school bus honks
and you run outside
with your lunch and backpack
to catch a ride

God loves you, sweet child.
Walk in peace.

When you fly down hill
on your trusted sled
moving so fast
that your nose turns red

God loves you, sweet child.
Walk in peace.

When deep in the jungle
the morning breeze
warms the branches
of the tropical trees

God loves you, sweet child.
Walk in peace.

When you twist and turn
and roll and flip
and jump and laugh
and run and skip,

or when jumping rope
to a steady beat
made by the stomping
of your hopping feet

God loves you, sweet child.
Walk in peace.

When you splish and splash
in the shallow tide
and look for shells
at the water's side

God loves you, sweet child.
Walk in peace.

When you're drawing and coloring
pictures that look
festive and bright
like the ones in this book

God loves you, sweet child.
Walk in peace.

When your back is straight
and you're walking tall
and you mustn't trip
or your load will fall,

or when you shop for food
on the market streets
then head for home
with some yummy treats

God loves you, sweet child.
Walk in peace.

When you swing so high
you can almost see
the squirrels at the top
of the maple tree

God loves you, sweet child.
Walk in peace.

When you sit and weave
in the afternoon
making lovely cloth
you'll be selling soon

God loves you, sweet child.
Walk in peace.

When you quietly fish
in the morning heat
so your family will have
plenty to eat,

or when you and your doll
dress up and pretend
that you're serving tea
to your mom and a friend

God loves you, sweet child.
Walk in peace.

While you're waiting for
all the rain to end
and you're keeping dry
with a trusted friend

God loves you, sweet child.
Walk in peace.

When you're climbing up
a steep mountainside
and reach the top
where the clouds collide

God loves you, sweet child.
Walk in peace.

When the sun is high
and the skies are light
when the world's aglow
and the day is bright

God loves you, sweet child.
Walk in peace.

The Author & Illustrator

Ingrid Hess teaches design at the University of Notre Dame. She is a graduate of Goshen College in Indiana, and trained in fine arts at Indiana University. Ingrid lives in South Bend. Her previous books include Praying With Our Feet, Sleep in Peace, and The Family Song.

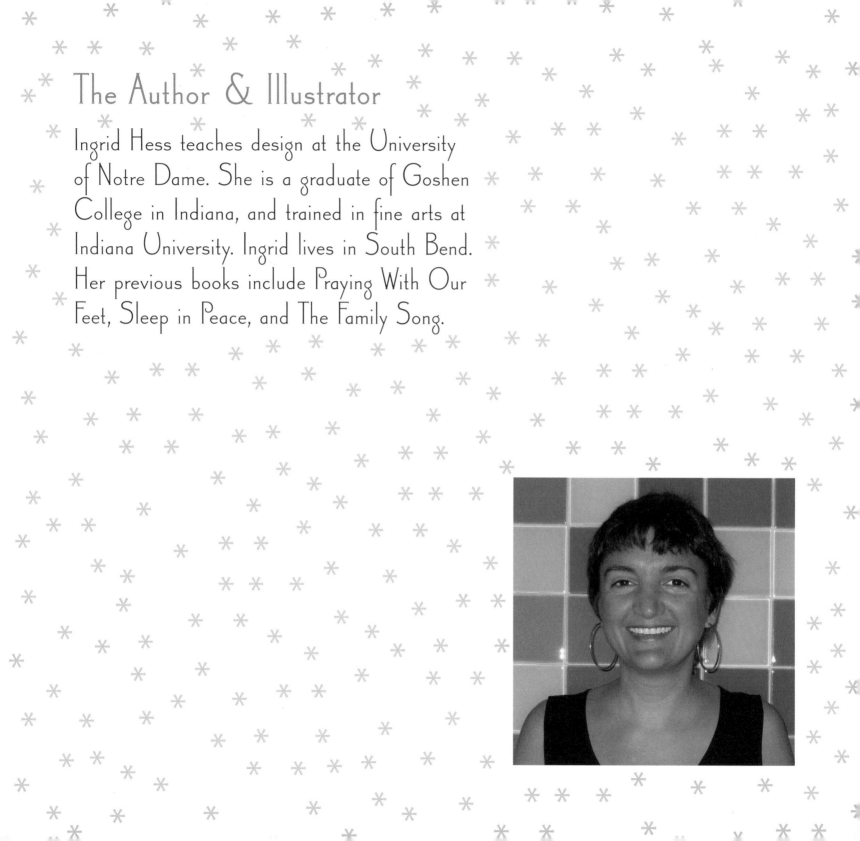